For Lola and Felix
C.D.

For Gustave and Jules
A.R.

First English edition published in 2015 by Berbay Publishing Pty Ltd
English translation © Berbay Publishing 2015

Bake Babushka! published in 2015 by Berbay Publishing Pty Ltd
PO Box 133
Kew East
Victoria 3102 Australia

First published by L'Atelier du Poisson Soluble 2005
Le Clafoutchka written by Celine Dupont and illustrated by Agnès Richter
The moral right of the author and illustrator has been asserted.

English adaptation by Michael Sedunary
Typesetting by Kylie Hall
Edited by Catherine McCredie
Printed and bound in China by Everbest Printing

National Library of Australia
Cataloguing-in publication data:
Dupont, Richter

Bake Babushka!
ISBN 978-0-9806711-7-9

Rise and shine!

It's a brand new day.

Time to get things under way...

It's the birthday of Ivan, my beautiful man, but things are not going according to plan.

I still haven't made my special Clafushka…

…and I'm out of cherries. I'm a bad babushka!

So off he goes!

Ivan reaches the road but he can't get across.

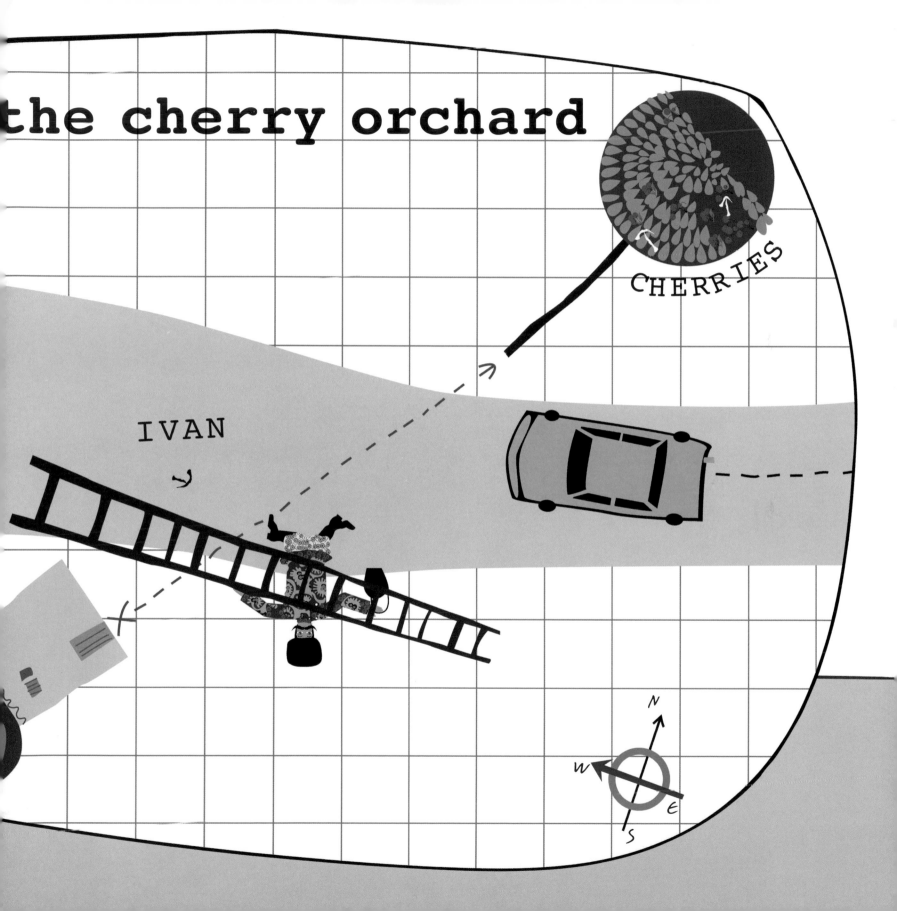

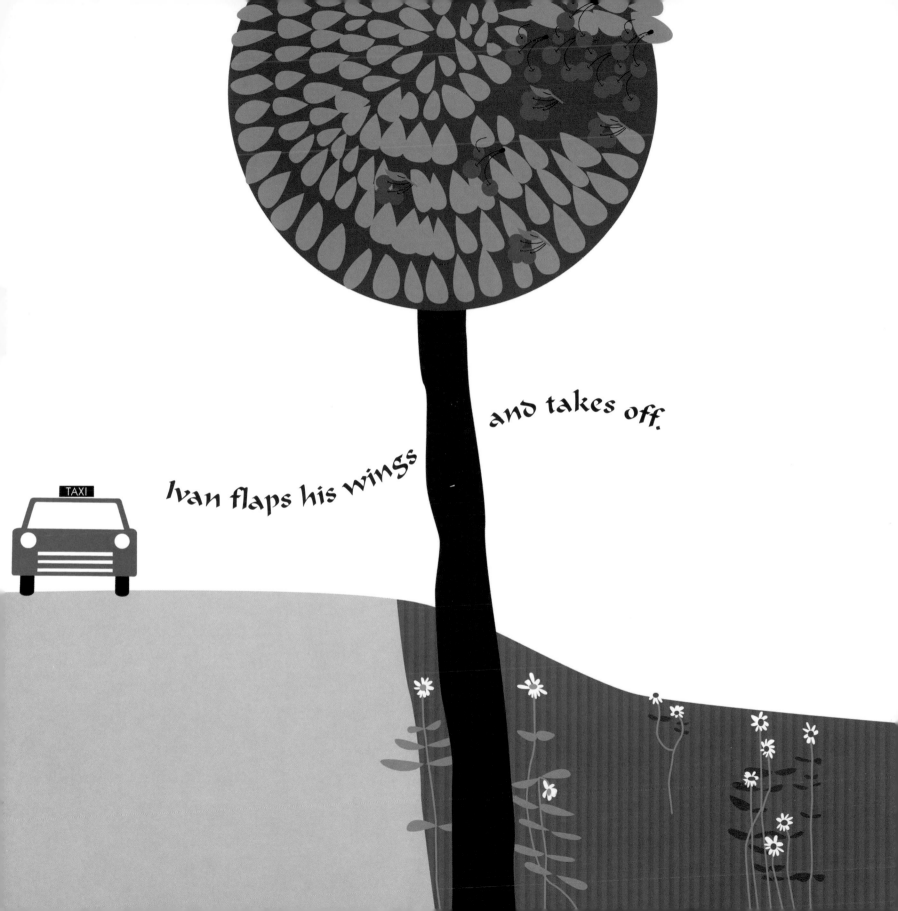

Ivan flaps his wings and takes off.

As you can see, all it takes to cross the road is a bit of clever thinking.

At last, the cherry tree!
Ivan climbs straight
to the top.

But don't worry, I won't rest.
I'm bringing sweet cherries
for the one I love best.

Better get across. It's almost noon.

It'll be too late if I'm not home soon.

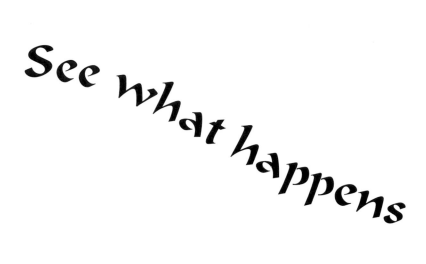

See what happens

when

By putting that piece there

with this piece here...

I've made

Ivan reappear.

Back home for the Clafushka.

I'll bake this cake as best I can.

A cherry cake, a fine Clafushka.
A very happy, proud babushka.

As for Ivan...
he's beside himself.

Babushka's recipe for Clafushka

I pour 80g (3/4 cup) of flour into a bowl and make a hollow in the middle.

I put in 100g (3/4 cup) of vanilla sugar, a pinch of salt, 2 eggs,

and 40g (1/3 cup) of cornflour. I mix these ingredients,